The BANANA SPLIT FROM OUTER SPACE

CATHERINE SIRACUSA

HYPERION BOOKS FOR CHILDREN

NEW YORK

To Sid, with love
— C.S.

Text and illustrations copyright © 1995 by Catherine Siracusa.
All rights reserved.
Printed in the United States of America.
For information address
Hyperion Books for Children,
114 Fifth Avenue, New York, New York 10011-5690.
FIRST EDITION
1 3 5 7 9 10 8 6 4 2

Library of Congress Cataloging-in-Publication Data

Siracusa, Catherine.
The banana split from outer space/Catherine Siracusa—1st ed.
p.   cm.
Summary: Stanley's ice-cream business suffers until he meets
Zelmo, an alien whose spaceship crash-lands on earth.
ISBN 0-7868-0040-2 (trade) — ISBN 0-7868-2033-0 (lib. bdg.)
ISBN 0-7868-1062-9 (pbk.)
[1. Ice cream, ices, etc. — Fiction.   2. Extraterrestrial beings —
Fiction.]   I. Title
PZ756215Ban   1995
[E] — dc20   94-6917   CIP   AC

The artwork for each picture is prepared using gouache, watercolor, pencil, and colored pencil.

CONTENTS

Stanley's Ice-Cream Stand

Everyone stopped at
Stanley's Ice-Cream Stand
on the road to town.

"I make the best ice cream," said
Stanley Pig. "Twenty-six flavors,
from apple swirl to zucchini nut."

Stanley was very busy.
Everyone loved his triple-dip
ice-cream cones, his hot fudge
butterscotch sundaes, his
chocolate mint marshmallow
malteds, and especially his
beautiful banana splits. "My
banana splits are out of this
world!" said Stanley.

Not too far from Stanley's a
big new highway was built. Now
it was the fastest way to get to
town.

"It doesn't matter," said
Stanley. "Everyone will still
come here because everyone
loves my ice cream."

But Stanley was wrong. Soon everyone drove the new highway. No one stopped at Stanley's anymore.

Stanley was very upset. "I need a new sign," he said. "Something very big and very bright. Something you can see from the new highway."

Stanley went into town. He bought wood and paint and other things to make his sign. Finally it was done.

"What a great sign!" said Stanley. "Now they'll see. Now they'll come back."

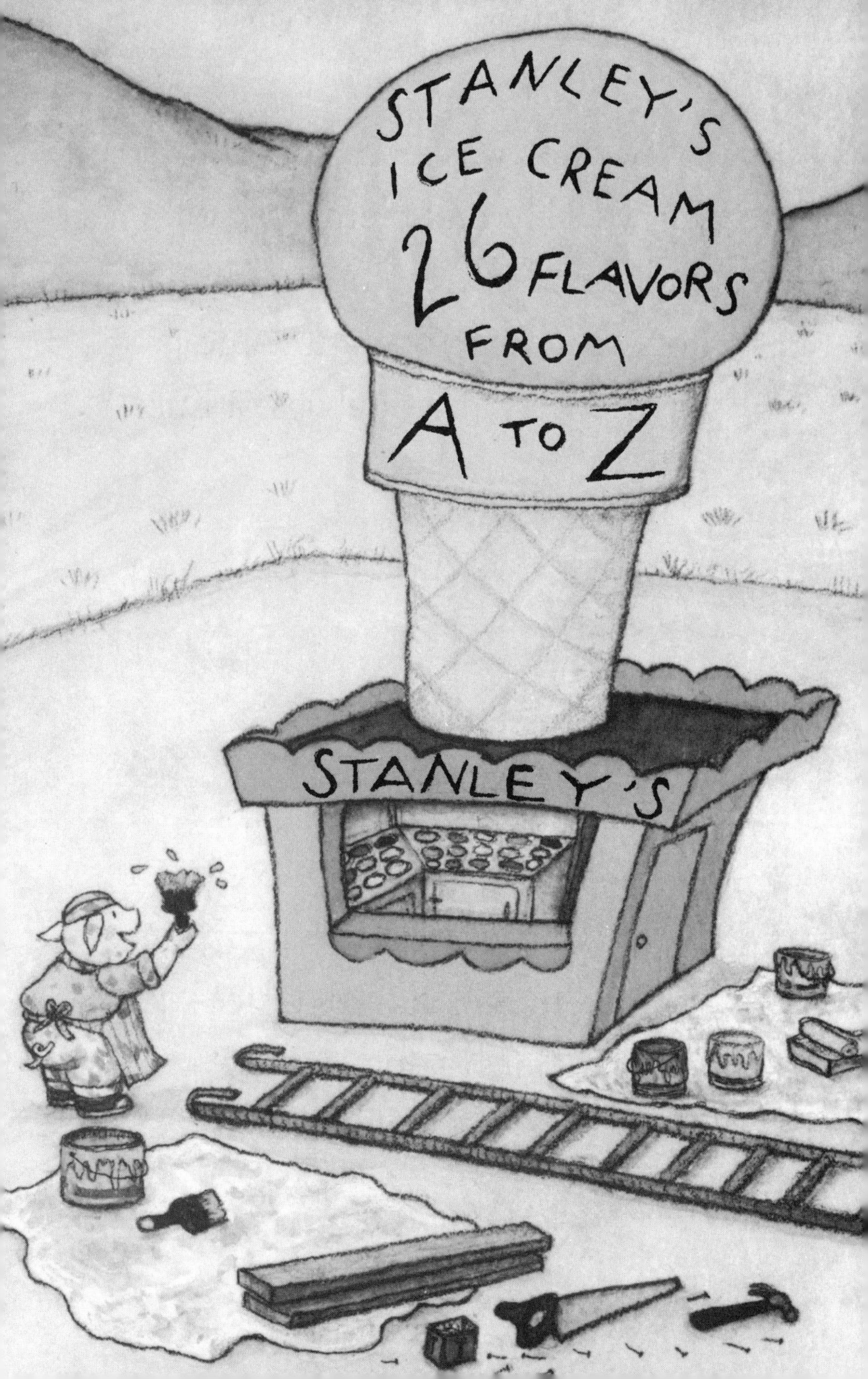
STANLEY'S
ICE CREAM
26 FLAVORS
FROM
A TO Z
STANLEY'S

Stanley was ready for a big crowd. He had plenty of hot fudge and butterscotch. He had lots of whipped cream, large jars of cherries, and big bags of nuts.

He had cones for ice-cream cones, bananas for banana splits, and twenty-six flavors of ice cream. But no one came.

"Where is everybody?" said Stanley.

Suddenly there was a big crash.
"What was *that?*" said Stanley.
It looked like a flying saucer.
He ran outside.

It was round and shiny. It sat
on top of his new sign.

2
Zelmo

"Hey! Get off my sign!" shouted Stanley.

"My saucer is stuck on your sign. I can't get down," said a strange voice from the saucer.

"I'll help you," said Stanley.

Stanley ran and got his ladder. A door opened in the saucer. A face looked out at Stanley.

"Greetings. I am Zelmo from Mars."

"You're a pig!" said Stanley. "Just like me, only green!"

He helped Zelmo down the ladder.

"I'm Stanley from Earth," he said.

"I am sorry about your sign, Stanley," said Zelmo. "I tried to land in your parking lot, but I missed."

"You must be tired," said
Stanley.

"I am tired. I am hungry," said
Zelmo. "I need ice cream."

"I never knew they ate ice cream on Mars," said Stanley.

"That is all we eat," said Zelmo. "I make ice cream on Mars, but we have only three flavors: fleenzil, uplaloo, and plinkee."

"Like chocolate, vanilla, and strawberry?" asked Stanley.

"Almost the same," said Zelmo. "I came to Earth to find new flavors for the Mars Ice-Cream Fair."

"You came to the right place," said Stanley.

Stanley and Zelmo went inside
the ice-cream stand.

"What would you like?" asked
Stanley.

"Vengo glop, please," said Zelmo.

"I don't have that," said
Stanley. "How about a banana
split instead?"

"Yes, please," said Zelmo.

Stanley made a big banana split
for Zelmo.

Zelmo ate it all in one big gulp.

"Good!" said Zelmo. "This is vengo glop! More, please."

Stanley made three more banana splits for Zelmo. Zelmo ate them all.

"More vengo glop, Zelmo?" asked Stanley.

"No thank you," said Zelmo. "Now I will make one for you."

"That is the most amazing banana split I've ever seen," said Stanley.

"This is how I make vengo glop on Mars," said Zelmo.

"You're good at this," said Stanley.

Zelmo sighed. "I wish I could fly my saucer as well as I make vengo glop."

Then Zelmo took some little things from his pocket and sprinkled them on top of his banana split.

"What's that?" asked Stanley.

"Floog," said Zelmo.

Stanley tasted some floog.
"Jelly beans!" he said. "Great idea! Vengo glop with floog! Your banana split is *really* out of this world!"

"You can sell it here," said
Zelmo. "Everyone will like it."
"I'll call it the banana split
from outer space!" said Stanley.

Then he shook his head. "It's
no good, Zelmo," said Stanley.
"No one comes here anymore."
"Why not?" asked Zelmo.
"Your ice cream is so tasty."

"Everyone used to stop here on the old road to town, but now they take the new highway," said Stanley.

"I thought they would see my new sign, but they go by so fast, they don't see it at all."

"I can help you, Stanley," said Zelmo. "Come with me."

3
Big Problems

Stanley and Zelmo went inside
the flying saucer.

"Wow!" said Stanley. "I never
saw anything like this!"

Zelmo pushed some buttons.
The saucer made a noise.

Bleep! Bleep! Bleep!

"That should work," said Zelmo.

Stanley and Zelmo went down the ladder.

Zelmo pushed a button on his belt. All the lights on the saucer flashed. The saucer made noises, too.

Bleep! Bleep! Bloing!

Bloing! Bloing! Bleep!

"Thanks, Zelmo!" said Stanley. "*Now* they will see my sign!"

Stanley and Zelmo waited and
waited and waited. And still no
one came.

"I don't understand," said
Stanley.

"They will come soon," said
Zelmo.

The saucer made a weird noise.
Bleep! Bloing! Blooie! Blonk!
Suddenly all the lights went out.
The saucer was dark and quiet.

"What happened?" asked
Stanley.

"I do not know," said Zelmo.
He hurried back to his saucer.

"Oh no! Oh no!" Zelmo cried.

"What is wrong?" asked
Stanley.

"I am out of dinko blam!" said
Zelmo.

"What's dinko blam?" asked
Stanley.

"It is my saucer fuel! It's all
gone!" said Zelmo.

"Now I will never get back to
Mars!"

Zelmo began to cry.

"Don't cry, Zelmo," said
Stanley.

Stanley and Zelmo were very
sad.

"We need something to cheer
us up," said Stanley. "This is the
last barrel of my grandpa's special
root beer."

He filled two mugs and gave
one to Zelmo. Zelmo drank it in
one gulp.

"ZOWIE!" shouted Zelmo.

"What's wrong?" asked Stanley.

"IT IS DINKO BLAM! IT IS
MY SAUCER FUEL!" shouted
Zelmo.

"Dinko blam is *root beer?*" asked
Stanley. "You *drink* your fuel?"

"Of course we drink it," said
Zelmo.

"You can go home now," said
Stanley. "Grandpa's root beer will
get you there."

"But then you will have no
more," said Zelmo.

"That's okay. I don't need it. No one comes here to buy root beer or anything," said Stanley.

"Why not come to Mars with me?" asked Zelmo. "We will have fun there."

"Let's go now!" said Stanley.

4

"Good-bye, Earth!"

STANLEY'S ICE CREAM 26 FLAVORS FROM A TO Z

They packed Zelmo's saucer with Stanley's twenty-six flavors of ice cream.

32

Stanley put on one of Zelmo's space suits. Then Stanley and Zelmo poured Grandpa's root beer into the saucer's fuel tank.

"Good-bye, ice-cream stand!" said Stanley. "Good-bye, Earth!"

"Fasten your seat belt," said Zelmo.

He pushed a blue button.

The saucer shook and shivered, but it didn't budge.

"What's wrong?" asked Stanley.

"I do not know," said Zelmo. "I am not very good at this."

"Don't give up, Zelmo," said Stanley.

34

Zelmo pushed the blue button again. The saucer took off. It went up. It went down. It spun around and around.

"I'm getting dizzy!" said Stanley.

"What is wrong now?" cried Zelmo.

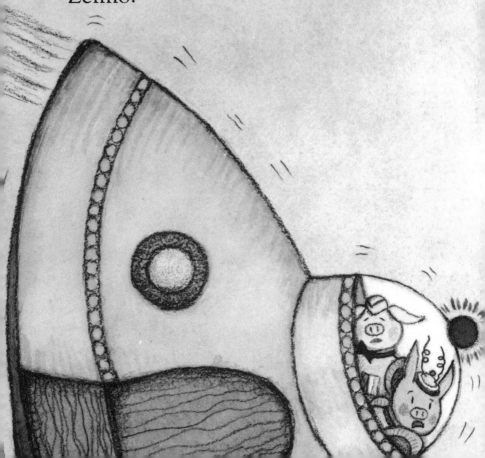

Stanley looked out the window.
"It's my ice-cream stand!" he said.
"It's stuck to your saucer!"

"Oh no!" cried Zelmo.

"You better find a place to
land," said Stanley.

"I'm afraid to land! Maybe we
will crash!" said Zelmo.

"Come on, Zelmo! You can do
it!" said Stanley.

Zelmo pushed all the buttons
on the saucer. Then he closed
his eyes.

The saucer landed with a
gentle thump.

"Open your eyes, Zelmo," said
Stanley.

"You did it! We landed!"

"Is everything okay?" asked
Zelmo.

"Let's go and see," said Stanley.

They climbed down the ladder.
"Great landing, Zelmo," said
Stanley. "Your saucer is fine. My
ice-cream stand is fine, too."

"I must be getting better," said
Zelmo.

They heard cars honking their horns.
"Look at all the cars," said Stanley.
"Where are we?" asked Zelmo.
"You moved my ice-cream stand to
the new highway!" said Stanley.
Cars began to stop.
"They want ice cream," said Stanley.
"Will you help me, Zelmo?"
"Of course," said Zelmo.

5
Stanley & Zelmo's

Now the ice-cream stand was a big success. Everyone wanted a banana split from outer space.

"Now everyone comes to Stanley's," said Zelmo.

"Stanley and *Zelmo's*," said Stanley. "We're partners."

"But I must go back to Mars now," said Zelmo. "It is almost time for the Mars Ice-Cream Fair. Will you come with me?"

"I can't come right now," said Stanley. "The ice-cream stand is too busy."

"I understand," said Zelmo.

Stanley helped Zelmo get ready
to go. He made sure that Zelmo's
saucer was not stuck to his sign.

"I will be back," said Zelmo.
"We will go to the Mars Ice-Cream
Fair next year. Good-bye, Stanley!
I will miss you!"

"Good-bye, Zelmo!" said
Stanley. "I'll miss you, too!"

The saucer took off. It
disappeared into the clouds.

"My sign needs some work now," said Stanley.

Soon it was all fixed up.

On top of his sign, Stanley built a flying saucer out of wood. He painted a picture of Zelmo waving from the saucer.

"Now I'll see Zelmo every day," said Stanley.

Stanley went inside the stand.
"I'm very hungry," he said.

So he made himself a vengo
glop with lots and lots of floog.